caillou®

The Missing Sock

Adaptation of the animated series: Sarah Margaret Johanson
Illustrations: CINAR Animation; adapted by Eric Sévigny

chouette **CINAR**®

D1529723

Mommy put a pile of freshly washed clothes on Caillou's bed.
"I need socks," Caillou said. He tossed the clothes around and finally pulled out one sock.
"Yay! My favorite!" he exclaimed as he put it on.

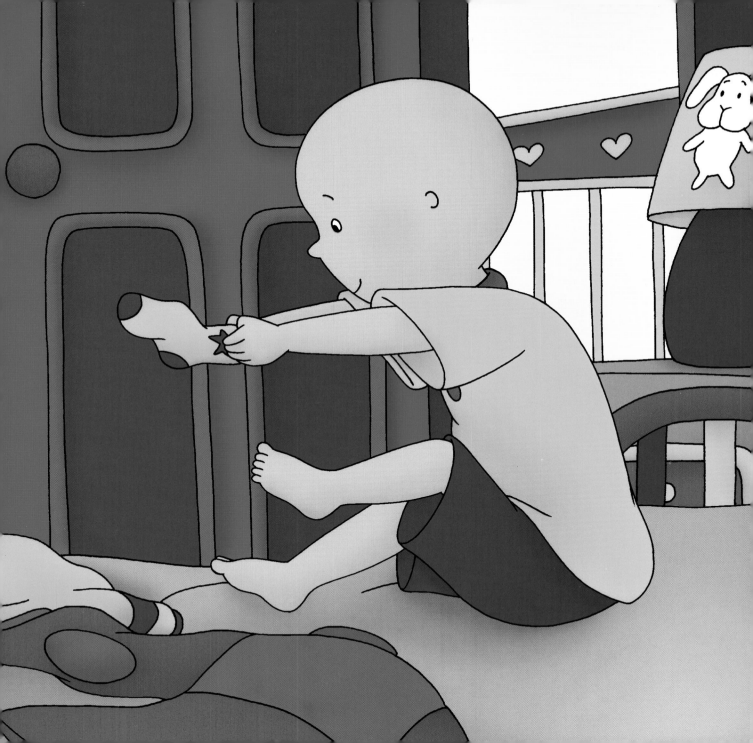

But where was the other sock? "Maybe it's in the laundry room," he said, and went downstairs to the basement. Caillou wanted to look in the washing machine but he wasn't tall enough.
He decided to go upstairs to get some help.

At the door of the
basement, Caillou
turned the knob.
To his surprise, it
came off in his hand!
"Oh, oh!" he said.
Caillou tried to push
the door open but it
didn't budge.
He was getting scared
and shouted:
"Mommy! Mommy!"

Caillou's daddy heard the shouting. "Caillou! It's OK, I'm here."

"Daddy, the door won't open!" Caillou said, sniffling.

"Don't worry, I'll get you out," Daddy said. "Did the doorknob come off on your side?"

"Yes, Daddy, it's in my hand."

Daddy turned the handle on his side very slowly.
The door opened and Caillou jumped into Daddy's arms.
"It's OK, Caillou. What were you doing down there?"
"Looking for my sock," Caillou said.
"Let's have another look together," Daddy suggested.

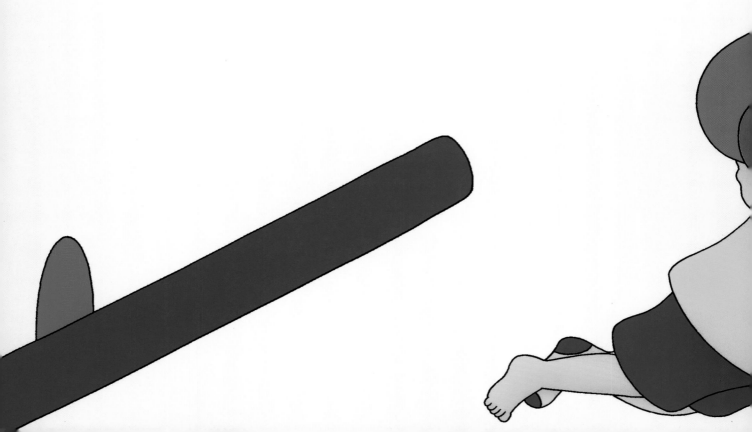

Caillou and Daddy went back downstairs to look for Caillou's missing sock.

Upstairs, Mommy was passing the basement door.

"Did I forget to close that?" she asked herself.

Mommy then closed the door and walked away.

Daddy and Caillou looked all around the laundry room.
They looked in the washing machine, and in the dryer too.
"Is it there, Caillou?"
"No Daddy, it's not here," Caillou replied.

"Well, let's find you another sock," Daddy said.
"But I want my favorite sock," Caillou exclaimed.
Daddy lifted Caillou up and started going
upstairs. "After we get you a pair of socks,
will you help me fix the doorknob?"
"OK," Caillou said.

At the top of the stairs,
Caillou and Daddy noticed
the door was closed.
"Oh, oh!" they both said.
"Let's call out together,"
Daddy suggested.
"Mommy! Mommy!"

Mommy came running.
"Oh dear!" she said. "Are
you stuck in there?"
And in no time at all, Mommy
managed to open the door.
"We should fix this right
away," Daddy said.
Mommy looked at Caillou's
bare foot and asked,
"Where's your sock?"
"I can't find it," Caillou
replied.

"Cheer up and look in that basket," Mommy said.
Caillou reached in and pulled out the missing sock.
"Here it is!" he exclaimed.
"OK, Caillou," Daddy said. "Let's fix this doorknob
so no one will ever get stuck in the basement again."

Text adapted by Sarah Margaret Johanson from the scenario of the
CAILLOU animated film series produced by CINAR Corporation
(© 1997 Caillou Productions Inc., a subsidiary of CINAR Corporation).
All rights reserved.
Original story written by Marie-France Landry.
Illustrations taken from the television series CAILLOU
and adapted by Eric Sévigny.
Art Direction: Monique Dupras

National Library of Canada cataloguing in publication

Johanson, Sarah Margaret, 1968 -
Caillou: the missing sock
(Clubhouse)
For children aged 3 and up.
Co-published by: CINAR Corporation.

ISBN 2-89450-445-4

1. Fear - Juvenile literature. 2. Claustrophobia - Juvenile literature.
3. Lost articles - Juvenile literature. I. CINAR Corporation. II. Title.
III. Title: Missing sock. IV. Series.

BF575.F2J64 2003   j152.4'6   C2003-940172-3

Legal deposit: 2003

We gratefully acknowledge the financial support
of BPIDP and SODEC for our publishing activities.

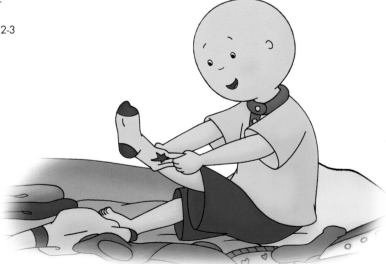

Printed in China
10 9 8 7 6 5 4 3 2 1